E LAURIA
Lauria, Lisa,
Doozers have bubble trouble /

Jim Henson's™

DOOZERS™
Have
Bubble Trouble

adapted by Lisa Lauria
based on the screenplay written by Craig Martin

Ready-to-Read

Simon Spotlight
New York   London   Toronto   Sydney   New Delhi

SIMON SPOTLIGHT
An imprint of Simon & Schuster Children's Publishing Division
1230 Avenue of the Americas, New York, New York 10020
This Simon Spotlight edition August 2019
© 2019 The Jim Henson Company. JIM HENSON'S mark & logo, DOOZERS mark & logo,
characters and elements are trademarks of The Jim Henson Company. All Rights Reserved.
All rights reserved, including the right of reproduction in whole or in part in any form.
SIMON SPOTLIGHT, READY-TO-READ, and colophon are registered trademarks of
Simon & Schuster, Inc.
For information about special discounts for bulk purchases, please contact Simon & Schuster
Special Sales at 1-866-506-1949 or business@simonandschuster.com.
Manufactured in the United States of America 0719 LAK
10 9 8 7 6 5 4 3 2 1
ISBN 978-1-5344-3197-3 (hc)
ISBN 978-1-5344-3196-6 (pbk)
ISBN 978-1-5344-3198-0 (eBook)

It is a busy day for
the Pod Squad.
They are cleaning
Doozer Depot.

"Thanks for helping me,"

Doozer Doodad says.

"We are happy to help,"

Molly Bolt says.

Flex is happy that they get
to try a new invention!

Doozer Doodad has a

super cleaning machine!

The Pod Squad cannot agree

on how to use it.

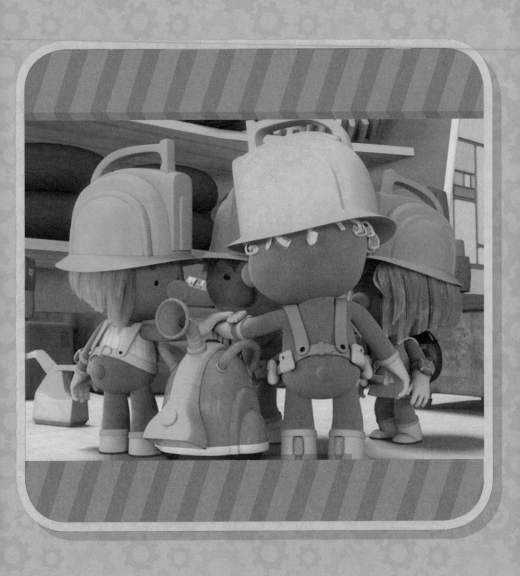

They reach for it at
the same time.

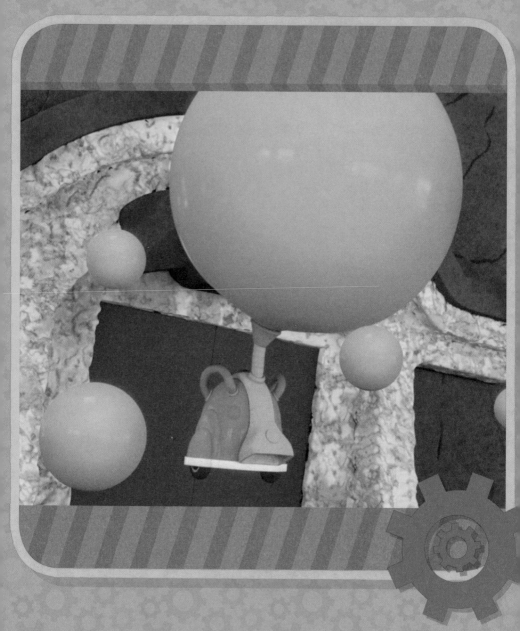

The machine breaks!

It starts to make bubbles.

The bubbles head toward

the bakery.

"Not in my bakery!"

Baker Timber Bolt says.

Then the bubbles head

toward the farm.

"Oh no!" Flex says.

"We need a plan,"

Molly Bolt says.

They go to

Professor Gimbal.

Molly Bolt tells him

that they broke the

machine.

Professor Gimbal

has an idea.

He shows them two ants

carrying a leaf.

"By working together,

they can lift the leaf,"

he says.

The Doozers try to pop

the bubbles again.

It does not work!

Professor Gimbal

has another machine.

It can pop bubbles!

"It will take days to pop

all the bubbles,"

Daisy Wheel says.

"Not if we work together!"

Flex says.

Everyone agrees.

They attach the machine
to the Podmobile.

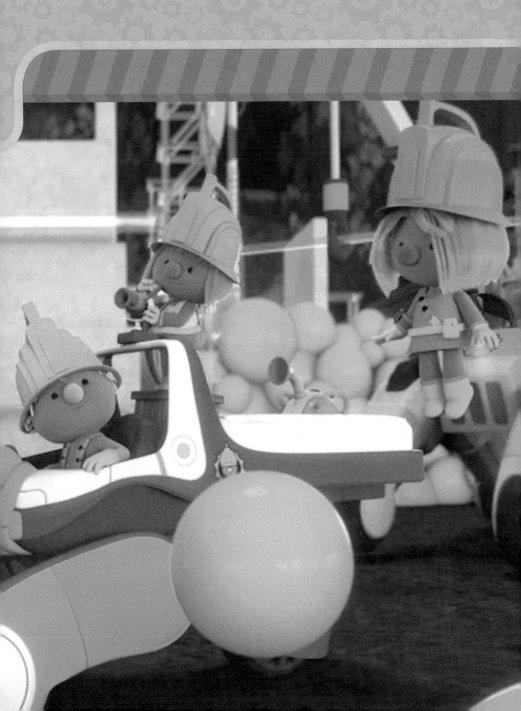

"Bubbles, we are
coming at you!"
Daisy Wheel says.

Soon, most of the

bubbles are gone!

The Pod Squad remembers
they meant to help
Doozer Doodad today!

Doozer Doodad is happy

they cleaned most of the mess.

He asks them to finish

popping the bubbles

in the Doozer Depot.

"There is nothing to it when you do, do, do it!" the Pod Squad cheers. They do it together!